FUNNY FIRSTS ™

LOVE STINKS

by Mike Thaler • pictures by Jared Lee

Troll

**For
Milton and Mitzi,
Jenny, Joshua, Nicky, Alex, and Ben—
Thalers all!**
M.T.

**To Bonnie Anderson,
my Natalie Applebaum.**
J.L.

FUNNY FIRSTS™ Mike Thaler and Jared Lee.
Text copyright © 1996 Mike Thaler.
Illustrations copyright © 1996 Jared Lee.
Published by WhistleStop, an imprint
and trademark of Troll Communications L.L.C.

Printed in the United States of America.

10 9 8 7 6 5 4 3 2 1

I'm in love with Natalie Applebaum.

I love her eyes.

I love her nose.

I love her ears.

I love her hair.

She sits in front of me in class.

I pull her hair.
She doesn't know I love her.

Someday I will tell her.
But I don't know how.

Should I tell her at recess on the jungle gym?
What if she kicks me?

Should I tell her on the phone?

What if she hangs up?

Should I write her a letter?

What if she tears it up?

Should I send her flowers?

Maybe she's allergic.

Should I send her candy?

Maybe she's on a diet.

Should I wait until Valentine's Day and give her a *big* card?

Then *everybody* will know.

Should I sneak her a little card?

Then she'll think I only love her a little.

Should I write her a poem?

Maybe she'll laugh at me.

Should I make her a drawing?

Maybe she'll hold her nose.

Should I sing her a song?
Maybe she'll hold her ears.
She has such pretty ears.

Yesterday, I was right behind her in the lunch line.
I was about to tell her.
Then somebody bumped my elbow,

and my Jell-O landed on her meatloaf.

At recess, I was on the swing next to hers.
I was going to tell her,
but when she swung up, I swung down.

I love her so much!
I'd do anything for her.
I'd slay dragons!

I'd climb mountains!

I'd eat spinach!

I want to marry her and go to the movies together.

But how can I tell her?
I love you, *Natalie*.
I love *you*, Natalie.
I *love* you, Natalie.
I say it over and over in my head.

"Snarvey Gooper," calls my teacher.
"Who was the third president of the United States?"

"I love you, Natalie," flies out of my mouth.

Oh, my gosh! I said it.
Now everybody knows.
Everybody's laughing.

Natalie's not laughing.
She's smiling at me.
She just winked.
Natalie loves me, too!

Doris Hopper isn't laughing, either.
She's smiling and winking, too.

She has nice eyes.
She has a nice nose.

She has nice ears.
She has nice hair.

I think I love her better than Natalie.

But how can I tell her?